JAN -- 2003

To Our Friends Throughout the World

The Mummer's Song

from

Bud Davidge & Ian Wallace

A GROUNDWOOD BOOK

AFTERWORD BY
KEVIN MAJOR

Douglas & McIntyre
Toronto Vancouver
Berkeley

This book is dedicated to my family —
Daphne, Chris and Janine
And to my mother and father Katie and Ev —
without whom there'd be no pictures of Bay du
Nord mummers forever in my mind — BD

To Ruby and Ed Kelly of Goose Bay who
'lowed the mummers in — IW

Text copyright © 1993 by Bud Davidge
Illustrations copyright © 1993 by Ian Wallace
Second printing 2002

Groundwood Books / Douglas & McIntyre
720 Bathurst Street, Suite 500, Toronto, Ontario M5S 2R4

Distributed in the USA by Publishers Group West
1700 Fourth Street, Berkeley, CA 94710

ONTARIO ARTS COUNCIL
CONSEIL DES ARTS DE L'ONTARIO

We acknowledge for their financial support of our publishing
program the Canada Council for the Arts, the Ontario Arts
Council and the government of Canada through the Book
Publishing Industry Development Program (BPIDP).

Canadian Cataloguing in Publication Data
Davidge, Bud
The mummer's song
ISBN 0-88899-178-9
I. Wallace, Ian. II. Title.
PS8557.A876M8 1993   jC813'.54   C93-093862-3
PZ7.D385Mu 1993

The illustrations are done in colored pencil on gray Canson paper.

Printed and bound in China

Don't seem like Christmas if the mummers are not here,
Granny would say as she knit in her chair.
Things have gone modern, I s'pose that's the cause.
Christmas is not like it was.

 Hark, what's the noise out by the porch door?
Granny, 'tis mummers, there's twenty or more.

Her old withered face brightens up with a grin.
Any mummers, nice mummers 'lowed in?

Come in, lovely mummers, don't bother the snow,
We can wipe up the water sure after you go.

Sit if you can or on some mummer's knee.
Let's see if we know who you be.

There's big ones and small ones and tall ones and thin,

Boys dressed as women and girls dressed as men,

Humps on their backs and mitts on their feet,

My blessed we'll die with the heat.

There's only one there that I think that I know,
That tall fellow standing o'er alongside the stove.

He's shaking his fist for to make me not tell.
Must be Willy from out on the hill.

Now that one's a stranger, if there ever was one
With his underwear stuffed and his trapdoor undone.

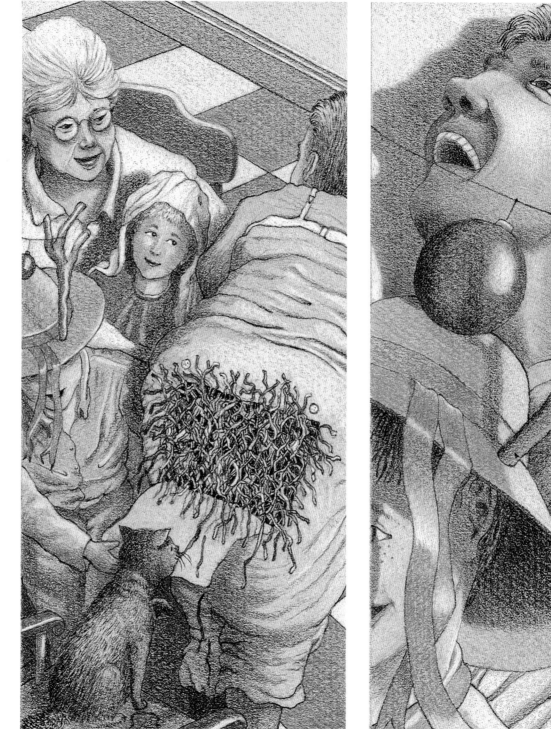

Is he wearing his mother's big forty-two bra?
I knows, but I'm not goin' t' say.

Don't s'pose you fine mummers would turn down a drop?
No, home brew or syrup, whatever you got.

Not the one with his rubber boots on the wrong feet,
He's had enough for to do him all week.

S'pose you can dance? Yes, they all nod their heads.

They've been tappin' their feet ever since they came in.

Now that the drinks have been all passed around

The mummers are planking 'er down.

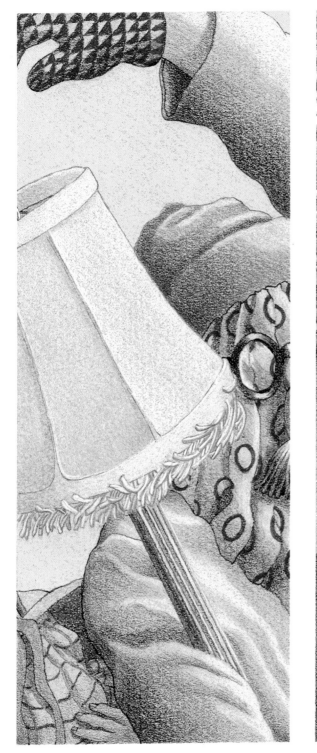
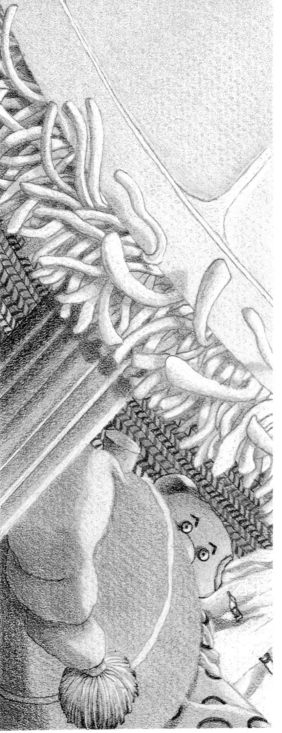

Be careful the lamp and hold onto the stove.

Don't swing Granny hard 'cause you know that she's old.

No need for to care how you buckles the floor

'Cause mummers have danced here before.

My God, how hot is it? We'd better go.
I allow we'll all get the devil's own cold.

Good night and good Christmas, mummers me dears.
Please God, we will see you next year.

 Good night and good Christmas, mummers me dears.

Please God, we will see you next year.

AFTERWORD

Christmas in rural Newfoundland can be a Christmas like no other. The excitement of the season continues long after the presents have been opened and the turkey dinner eaten, for the Twelve Days of Christmas (from December 26 to January 6) is the time for mummering.

A rough knock on your door after dark probably means that mummers are about. You open the door and there stands a swarm of people in outlandish disguises, one cawing out a request to be let in, all acting like proper fools. They trail into the house, eager for a good bit of sport. They tease and joke and you prod and poke,

but you're still confounded as to just who they might be. They are no doubt neighbors and friends, or someone visiting from up the coast, but it's a guessing game, to be sure. If you're right, then off comes the mask. Now one of them is anxious for a dance, so another starts up a tune on the accordion or fiddle. Soon they're steppin' 'er out so hard you wonder if the floor can stand it. They'll have a drink and perhaps a bit of fruitcake before they go, and then they're out the door as quickly as they came in, off to take their Christmas cheer to other fun-loving souls just down the road.

House visits like this one have been part of the

Newfoundland Christmas since at least the early 1800s, as settlers to the Island brought with them their many folk traditions from West Country England and southern Ireland. For those early settlers and their descendants, Christmas was the one time of the year when work was set aside and merrymaking took its place.

As the way of life changed, especially in recent decades, mummering became less widespread than it once was. It remained strongest in the more remote communities along Newfoundland's coast. However, with new generations more aware of their heritage, mummering has undergone somewhat of a revival. This is due in no small part to the immense popularity of "The Mummer's Song," first released by Bud Davidge and Sim Savoury in December 1983. It would seem mummering is in no danger of disappearing, as many might have predicted. Rather, it is alive and hardy, with "The Mummer's Song" now a musical focal point of a marvellous tradition.

— *Kevin Major*

NOTE
planking 'er down — dancing wildly
syrup — sugary drink for children that is mixed with water